For the urban foxes who remind us
that we are wild things too.—G.L

For all the little Wildthings,
especially my own.—R.B

OXFORD
UNIVERSITY PRESS

Great Clarendon Street, Oxford OX2 6DP
Oxford University Press is a department of the University of Oxford.
It furthers the University's objective of excellence in research, scholarship,
and education by publishing worldwide. Oxford is a registered trade mark
of Oxford University Press in the UK and in certain other countries

Text copyright © Gill Lewis 2020
Illustrations copyright © Rebecca Bagley 2020

The moral rights of the author have been asserted

Database right Oxford University Press (maker)

First published 2020

British Library Cataloguing in Publication Data

Data available

ISBN 978-0-19-277176-6

1 3 5 7 9 10 8 6 4 2

Printed in China

Paper used in the production of this book is a natural,
recyclable product made from wood grown in sustainable forests.
The manufacturing process conforms to the environmental
regulations of the country of origin.

Willow Wildthing
and the
Dragon's Egg

Written by Gill Lewis
Illustrated by Rebecca Bagley

OXFORD
UNIVERSITY PRESS

Contents

Chapter 1

Trouble in the Wilderness ... 9

Chapter 2

The Invisible Tribe ... 20

Chapter 3

The Disappearance of Mouse ... 32

Chapter 4

Faces in the Forest ... 39

Chapter 5

Terms and Conditions Apply ... 51

Chapter 6

Land of the Dragon . . . 59

Chapter 7

When the Singing Stops . . . 70

Chapter 8

Power of the Egg . . . 81

Chapter 9

No Place for Dragons . . . 91

Chapter 10

The Old Magic . . . 97

Chapter 11

Releasing the Dragon . . . 108

Chapter 1
Trouble in the Wilderness

It isn't every day that a dragon turns up in the
garden.

Willow's brother, Freddie, found it. He and
Willow had been searching for fossils in the soil
where Dad had been digging. Dad was clearing a
space for a summer house.

Freddie cupped his hands around something
small that wriggled inside his fingers. 'Dragon,
dragon, dragon!' he yelled.

'Let's see,' said Willow.

Freddie shook his head and held it against his chest. 'Mine.'

Freddie was three years old. He loved dragons. His favourite toy was a fluffy pink dragon that Willow had given him for his second birthday.

'I won't take it,' said Willow. 'I just want to look at it.'

Freddie slowly uncurled his fingers. 'Dragon,' he whispered.

Willow peered at it. It did look a bit like a very

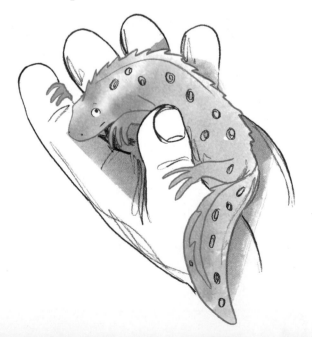

small dragon. It was long, thin, and wriggly, with four squat legs and feet that gripped onto Freddie's fingers. It had a crest from the top of its head all the way down its back to the end of its long tail.

'It hasn't got any wings,' said Willow.

'It's a baby dragon,' said Freddie.

Willow wondered if it might be a lizard, but it didn't have any scales. It was soft and squidgy and slightly damp. 'Let's show Dad.'

Dad was having a tea break with Nana on the bench outside the back door. Nana had made Willow's favourite triple chocolate-chip cookies.

Freddie proudly plopped the baby dragon on Nana's lap. 'Dragon!' he said.

Nana took one look and screamed. 'Ugh!' She flicked it away and it flew through the air, landing on the patio.

Freddie saw Nana's horrified face and covered

his eyes and howled too. Then Sniff, Willow's dog, rushed outside, barking and joining in with all the noise.

'It's OK,' Willow said. She scooped Freddie's dragon in her hands. 'Look, Freddie. I've found it. It's not hurt.'

Sniff tried to look too, but Willow pushed him away.

Freddie peered at it through his fingers.

'Take it away,' said Nana. 'It's dirty. You'll have to wash your hands now.'

'It's Freddie's dragon,' said Willow. She held it out for Freddie, but he shook his head.

'Dirty,' he said.

Dad looked over her shoulder. 'I think it's a newt. An amphibian. A bit like a frog.'

'Put it back,' said Nana. 'You know Freddie has to be careful not to pick up germs.'

Freddie had been poorly since he was born and sometimes needed time in hospital. It's why Willow and her family had moved to the new house in the new town, to be closer to the hospital. The doctors said Freddie had to be careful not to pick up coughs and colds. Willow's mum and dad were always trying to keep things clean.

'It's clean dirt,' said Willow.

'There's no such thing as clean dirt,' said Nana, whose own cupboards were full of the latest cleaning products. 'Take it away. You'll have to wash your hands now if you want a cookie.'

Willow sighed. 'Come on, Freddie,' she said. 'Show us where you found it.'

Freddie didn't want to hold his dragon again, but he led Dad and Willow down the garden. The last owner of the house hadn't done anything with the garden for years, and the grass was so long that it came up to Willow's waist. The bushes were overgrown and tangled with brambles and ivy. Nettles grew in thick green clumps and bindweed curled around the washing line.

Mr Snow, the neighbour, put his head over the fence. 'Afternoon,' he said. 'Good to see this place having a tidy-up at last.'

Dad grinned. 'It's a bit of a jungle. We'll soon sort it out.'

Willow walked on, and when Mr Snow was out of earshot, she turned to Dad. 'I like it wild like this,' she said. 'Can't we keep it like this for me and Freddie?'

Dad smiled and nodded his head towards Mr Snow. 'Not everyone likes a jungle. It is a bit of a mess, and we need to clear these weeds.'

Willow sighed. 'Where did you find your dragon, Freddie?'

'There,' said Freddie. He pointed to the ground where Dad had been digging.

Willow just stared at some of the empty spaces where the bushes had been pulled up. She turned to Dad. 'We can't pull up all the bushes. Freddie's dragon lives beneath them.'

'I'm sure there are plenty of other places for it to live,' said Dad. 'I think newts like damp places near ponds.'

Willow looked around. The neighbours' gardens had patios and tiny squares of cut grass. Not a flower was out of place and it looked like weeds were forbidden. They didn't have ponds either. 'Where will it go if we dig up its home? It has to have somewhere to live.'

'My dragon,' said Freddie, peering into Willow's hand.

'I've got an idea,' said Dad. 'Wait here.'

While Willow waited, she looked closely at the newt in her hand. It turned its head to the side and its beady little eyes looked up at her.

Freddie touched it gently with his finger. 'Dirty?' he asked.

'No,' said Willow. 'Here, you hold it.' She passed him the newt and Freddie wrinkled up his nose as the newt crawled across his hands.

'Tickles,' he said.

Willow laughed. 'We'll call him Mr Tickles.'

Dad arrived back with a large glass tank. 'I knew I had my old fish tank somewhere. We can make a home for it in here. Freddie will be able to look at it any time he wants to.'

Willow helped Dad scoop soil, some old leaves, and some stones into the fish tank.

'We'll put in a bowl of water like a small pond,' said Dad.

'Zoo,' said Freddie.

'Yes,' laughed Dad. 'Yes, you have your very own zoo now.'

Mum came down the garden and inspected Mr Tickles in his new tank. 'Come on, Freddie. It's your afternoon nap time. She lifted Freddie up into her arms and Dad picked up the tank with Mr Tickles.

Willow watched them walk back to the house and sighed. There was no one to play with now. 'Come on, Sniff,' she called. But Sniff was sniffing at the hedge at the bottom of the garden, his tail wagging furiously. 'What is it, Sniff?'

Something flew over the hedge and landed with a plop at her feet.

Willow picked it up. It was a crumpled piece of paper, screwed up in a tight ball. She carefully opened it out and read the message scrawled on the paper: *Trouble in the Wilderness. Come now!*

Below the words were four different paw prints and a feather.

Fox, Bear, Hare, Mouse, and Raven.

Willow's heart skipped a beat.

This was a call to the Wilderness.

The Wild Things were in trouble and needed her help.

Chapter 2
The Invisible Tribe

Willow shoved the piece of paper into her pocket and ran to the house. 'I'm taking Sniff for a walk to meet some friends,' she yelled. She filled a tin with some cookies and stuffed it in her rucksack.

'Don't be long,' called Mum.

But Willow was already on her way out of the house, her feet flying across the grass. Sniff ran by her side, barking. Sniff was Willow's dog. He had come from the dog rescue centre. He had one eye, wonky teeth, and a brave heart. No one had

wanted him. But the moment Willow saw him,
she just knew they belonged together. Sniff loved
Willow more than anything in the world.

Willow and Sniff scrambled under the hedge to
see two figures crouching on the other side. They
were two children she recognized.

The taller one stood up and brushed dirt from
her knees. She was a girl a bit older than Willow,
with jet-black hair and a jet-black cloak with
frayed edges.

'Raven!' said Willow.

'Willow Wildthing, what kept you?' said Raven.
She flapped her cloak impatiently.

The smaller figure flung his arms around Sniff,
and Sniff licked his nose.

'Mouse, you're here too,' said Willow. Mouse
and Raven were two of the Wild Things. 'Where
are the others?'

'They're back at River Camp,' said Raven. 'Come on, there's no time to lose. There are strangers in the Wilderness.'

'An enemy tribe,' added Mouse. 'They keep stealing things from us.'

Willow had met the Wild Things before when she had followed them into the scrubby patch of woodland behind her garden. She had joined them on an adventure and become a Wild Thing too.

The woodland had once been the gardens and grounds of an old house that had burned down long ago. It was now overgrown with weeds and trees. Roads and houses had been built all around it. It was a small patch of green in the grey concrete town. Adults said it was a mess and needed clearing out, but deep inside it held a secret. It wasn't a wasteland; it held the

Wilderness, where time stretched, where rivers ran deep, and giant forests grew. It was a place where anything could happen. Outside the Wilderness, the Wild Things looked like any other children, but the Wilderness had a curious effect on them. They became a mixture of wild creature and child.

No one else knew about the Wilderness.

It was their secret place.

No one else went there.

No one else, until now.

Willow and Sniff raced along behind Raven and Mouse. They ran along the path at the end of the gardens until they reached a plank over the ditch of green stagnant water. The Green Slime River marked the boundary of the Wilderness. They kicked off their shoes, walked across the plank, and pulled it up after them so no one could follow.

Willow scrunched her toes into the dry leaves and dirt and smiled. It was good to be back in the Wilderness. Insects hovered and danced in shafts of golden sunlight like fairy dust.

The air seemed to sparkle with magic. She looked across at her friends. They seemed to change too. Raven's cloak gleamed with shiny blue-black feathers. Mouse twitched his nose and he scurried away to a dark tunnel through the undergrowth. It was the Holloway, a tunnel made from the feet of forest animals through the thorns and brambles. It was the secret entrance that led deep into the Wilderness.

'Come on,' said Mouse.

Willow followed them, crawling on her hands and knees until the tunnel opened out onto a steep wooded slope. She stood up and brushed the dirt from her jeans. Her hands and feet were muddy,

'You remember we had things going missing last time we were here?' said Fox. 'I lost my penknife and Hare lost her compass.'

Willow nodded.

'Other things have gone missing too,' said Hare. 'They've taken our pots and pans. We can't make hot chocolate.'

'Some of my ropes have gone,' said Fox.

'And my bird book,' said Raven. 'This morning I had it next to me on this bench. Then they took it.'

'Who are "they"?' said Willow.

'That's just it,' said Hare. 'They took it right from underneath our noses. We didn't even see them do it.'

'They're invisible,' whispered Mouse. 'The Invisible Tribe.'

Willow shivered and looked around her. Her

spine tingled. 'How do we know they're not here now, standing next to us?'

Raven nodded. 'We thought of that, and that's why we need Sniff.'

Sniff looked up and barked.

'Sniff will smell them coming and warn us,' said Raven. 'We need to catch them. We need to set a trap.'

Fox nodded. 'We could put the cookies out as bait . . .'

'Not the cookies,' said Bear. 'I'm starving.'

'They won't get them,' said Raven, 'because we'll be lying in wait. We need to pretend to be out, but we'll hide around here and wait for them to come.'

'Good idea,' said Fox. 'We need to cover all entrances to River Camp. Raven and I will hide across the river under those bushes.'

'And Willow and I will hide behind those rocks over there,' said Hare.

'I'm not going far from those cookies,' said Bear. 'I'm hiding inside the den. I'll catch whoever tries to take them from us.'

'I'll hide with you,' said Mouse.

And so the Wild Things left the cookies in full view on the fallen log. Then they pretended to leave the camp, but instead they ducked down in their hiding places.

Willow crouched low, holding Sniff in her arms.

The sun sank a little lower behind the trees.

Birds came down to dust themselves in the clearing.

All was quiet and still.

The Wild Things waited,

and waited,

and waited.

Just as Willow's eyes began to close, she felt a growl rise in Sniff's chest.

He sniffed the air. 'Uff!' he warned softly. 'Uff!'

The birds in the clearing suddenly scattered up into the trees.

Sniff's growl grew louder and louder.

Willow stared out to River Camp, but she couldn't see anyone or anything out there at all.

Chapter 3
The Disappearance of Mouse

Willow nudged Hare who had been snoozing too. 'Something's out there,' she whispered.

They both peered above the rocks to look at River Camp. The tin of cookies was on the fallen log, untouched. The camp was quiet and still. Too still maybe, Willow thought.

Sniff growled again.

Something was different, but Willow couldn't work out what it was. The river gurgled and looped around the camp. It glittered in the sunlight that filtered through the trees. At the edge of the camp, the leaves of a small bush trembled in the breeze.

Nothing else moved.

Willow frowned. She looked up at the branches above her. Not a leaf stirred. The clouds hung motionless in the sky.

That was strange.

There was no wind.

There was no breeze.

Willow looked back at the bush again. Its leaves were definitely quivering. Come to think of it, she wasn't sure she'd seen a bush there before. As she watched, the bush moved sideways. She blinked and looked again. Yes, it was moving so slowly it was barely noticeable, but it was creeping stealthily towards the cookie tin.

Willow shot up from her hiding place. 'It's there!' she yelled. 'That bush.'

Hare tried to pull her down. 'Are you mad? What are you doing?'

'It's the bush!' yelled Willow. 'Catch it!'

The bush leapt over to the fallen log and then sprinted away on a pair of skinny stick legs, taking the cookie tin with it.

A roar bellowed from the den and Bear burst out, chasing the bush. Willow and Hare followed with Sniff barking alongside them. Raven and Fox

jumped out from their hiding place too, and the
Wild Things chased the bush, following it into the
Forest of Forever Night.

They ran further and further into the forest,
tripping and stumbling over tree roots. The trees
grew taller and closer together. In the green gloom,
it soon became difficult to see.

The Wild Things stopped and looked around
them. The bush had disappeared from sight.

'It went this way,' called Bear.

'No, this way,' shouted Fox.

'I heard it over here,' called Raven.

'How do we find a bush in the middle of a forest?' said Hare.

'Well, if we can't see it, Sniff can sniff it out,' said Willow. 'Go on, Sniff.'

Sniff put his nose to the ground, trotting in circles until he followed a scent to a tree with low branches. 'Uff!' he barked, looking up into the tree.

The Wild Things gathered below the tree and looked up. A long rope hung from a branch. It was swinging back and forth as if something or someone had swung away from them through the trees.

Raven tried to follow along the ground, but the undergrowth was dense and thorny and held her back.

'Sniff can't follow the scent now,' said Willow.

Fox kicked the ground. 'We lost them,' he said.

'Worse than that,' said Bear, sitting down.
'They've got our cookies.'

'Let's get back,' said Fox. 'We'll need to come up
with another plan.'

'How do you catch a bush?' asked Hare.

'We should have made a proper trap,' said
Raven. 'A deep pit covered with leaves.'

Willow walked back to camp with the others.
She looked around. 'Where's Mouse?' she said.

'He was asleep when the thief came,' said Bear,
sitting down and rubbing his belly. 'I'm hungry. I
wish we hadn't left all the cookies in the tin.'

Hare lifted the flap to the den. 'Come out,
Mouse. The thief has been and gone. We didn't
catch them.'

Poor Mouse, thought Willow. He must have been terrified to have been left on his own.

'Mouse?' said Hare, sticking her head inside the den. 'Mouse, are you there?'

Willow looked up. Hare slipped into the den, and there was silence followed by a soft gasp.

'Oh no,' said Hare. She came out holding a note and something small cupped in her hand.

The others turned to look at her.

'What is it?' said Raven.

'Mouse is gone,' said Hare grimly. 'He's been taken by the Invisible Tribe.'

Chapter 4
Faces in the Forest

The other Wild Things followed Hare into the den. Willow knelt down on Mouse's blanket. It was still warm from where he had been lying.

'I found this here,' said Hare. She opened her hand to show a small model shaped from mud. Twigs had been pressed into the mud to look like whiskers and a tail. It was a model of Mouse. 'And there's a note,' she said.

Raven took the note from Hare's hand and held it in the shaft of light coming through the den.

The paper had been torn from one of the Wild Things' notebooks, and the message looked like it had been hastily scrawled in messy handwriting.

'What does it say?' said Fox.

'*If you want Mouse back*,' Raven read, '*meet us at the Lake of the Dead. Terms and conditions apply.*'

'The Lake of the Dead,' said Fox, grimly.

'Terms and conditions apply?' said Bear. 'What does that mean?'

'I don't know, but we're going to find out,' said Hare. She paced in circles. 'The Lake of the Dead must be somewhere in the Forest of Forever Night. We haven't explored far into the forest before.'

'Does it say anything else?' said Willow.

Raven turned the note over in her hands and peered closely at the writing on the other side. '*P.S. Follow the cookie crumbs.*'

'Follow the cookie crumbs?' said Bear. 'Our

cookies! They'll be eaten by birds.'

Fox stared at the note. 'The Invisible Tribe must have left a trail for us to follow.'

Raven nodded. 'They must know the crumbs will be taken by birds, and so we won't find it if we try to get there again.'

Hare smiled. 'A map-maker can always find the way.' She bounded over to the bench and reached deep inside the hollow log. She pulled out a long cardboard tube and opened the top and looked inside. 'They haven't found the map,' she said. Hare was the map-maker. She had drawn a map of the Wilderness, but there were places where even the Wild Things had never been. 'It's time for us to discover the Forest of Forever Night.'

'Come on,' said Raven. 'There's no time to lose. We must find Mouse.'

The Wild Things stood at the edge of the

Forest of Forever Night in solemn silence. They
had never entered deep into the forest before.
The trees in the woodland around River Camp
had wide spreading branches where golden
dappled light fell to the ground. But in the Forest
of Forever Night, the trees grew tall and close
together, so close that hardly any light shone
through. It was as if daylight had a dimmer switch.
Damp ferns and mosses sprouted between rocks
and tree roots.

It was the forest of dark fairy tales.

It was the forest of the Invisible Tribe.

'Look,' said Hare. 'A trail of crumbs.'

The Wild Things looked at the ground where
a line of cookie crumbs disappeared under a low
branch. Willow had to hold onto Sniff to stop him
eating them. They crawled under the branch into a
space where mosses and grass had been trampled,

as if someone—or something—had been lying there.

Fox looked back at their camp. 'There's a good view of the camp from here,' he whispered 'This is where they've been spying on us. There must be more than one of them.'

Willow shivered. She didn't like the thought of being watched.

Raven nodded. 'They must've been watching us all the time.'

'And some of them grabbed Mouse while we were chasing one of the others,' said Bear.

The hairs on Willow's arms rose. 'How many do you think there are?' she whispered.

Hare crouched down and traced her hands in the mud. 'Difficult to tell,' she said. 'There are footprints. Small human footprints. Lots of them.'

'What are we going to do?' said Bear.

'There's only one thing we can do,' said Raven. 'We have to follow them.'

The Wild Things followed the crumbs into the forest. A path seemed to open up, and whether it had been made by wild animals or the Invisible Tribe, it was impossible to tell. Hare stopped from time to time to sketch the path on the map to mark distinctive rocks or unusual shaped trees. She traced the path north on the map.

Willow peered over her shoulder. 'How can you tell we're going north?'

'Look closely,' said Hare. 'The moss grows more on the wetter north side of the tree trunks.'

Willow began to notice that all the tree trunks were different. She walked from tree to tree, running her hands along the rough bark. She had never really thought about trees as living things before. Were they like people? Did they think and feel like she could? Could they tell she was here? She could feel the hairs on the back of her neck begin to rise. It felt as if all the trees in the forest were watching her. She imagined a face and eyes staring out at her from each tree.

She blinked and looked back. There *was* a face staring at her. It seemed to be a part of the tree, level with her own face. It had a nose and mouth and a pair of luminous eyes looking right at her.

Willow gasped.

'What?' said Raven.

'A face,' said Willow. 'There.'

Bear backed into her. 'And there,' he said, pointing at another tree.

As they looked, they began to notice all the trees along the path had faces.

'It's just mud,' said Raven, touching one face. 'Someone has made these. And they've painted pebbles with luminous paint for eyes.'

The Wild Things walked on in silence, past more staring mud-faces in the forest. Even Sniff kept close to Willow and didn't seem to want to wander far like he usually did.

'Grrr!' said Sniff, backing away from one tree. The tree was small, a sapling with bushy branches.

'Come on, Sniff,' said Willow.

But Sniff kept growling.

Willow stopped and looked at the face. The mud had been applied smoothly across the forehead and cheeks. This one's eyes were shut. Willow peered closer, her face almost touching the tree face.

Sniff growled again.

'It's only a tree,' said Willow. She was trying to convince herself as much as Sniff.

But she was wrong.

The tree's eyes snapped open.

Willow screamed and stumbled backwards.

The tree laughed, jumped into the shadows, and was gone.

Willow ran after the others with Sniff barking at her heels. 'The trees are watching us!' she shouted. She caught up with them in a small clearing where the trees had thinned out around a pool of dark water.

On the far side of the pool, there was a huge tree, much bigger than the other trees. It had gnarled roots, like large clawed feet, and long branches that swept low to the ground. On one of the branches sat Mouse.

'Mouse!' called Raven.

Mouse looked up. 'You're here.'

'Come down,' said Fox.

'I can't,' said Mouse.

'It's not far to jump,' called Raven. 'We'll catch you.'

'It's not that,' shouted Mouse. 'If I move, the Ogre Tree will get me.'

'The what?' said Fox.

'This tree, the Ogre Tree,' said Mouse.

'Says who?' said Hare.

'Says us,' said a voice.

The Wild Things turned to see a figure step out into the clearing. Willow recognized the face as the one she had seen in the small tree. It was a boy with twigs and leaves tied on to camouflage clothes.

The Invisible Tribe had just become visible.

Chapter 5
Terms and Conditions Apply

A cloud passed overhead, and shadows shifted. As quickly as he had appeared, the boy was gone.

Raven spun around. 'Where did he go?'

'Over here,' said a voice.

The Wild Things turned to see the boy on the far side of the Lake of the Dead.

Fox frowned. He wasn't sure if it was the same boy. 'How did you get there?'

'Forest magic,' said the boy.

Another voice spoke, a girl's this time. She

stepped out into the clearing. She was taller than the boy, with a wild mane of hair. Her face was painted with mud, and she also wore camouflage-print clothes with twigs and leaves attached. She put her hands on her hips and glared at the Wild Things.

'Who are you?' said Raven.

'We're the Bark Skins,' said the girl.

'Well, we're the Wild Things,' said Raven.

'We know,' said the girl. 'We know everything in the forest. We are the forest.'

Raven took a step towards her. 'We want Mouse back,' she said.

'Only on one condition,' said the girl.

Raven narrowed her eyes. 'What condition?'

'That you let us have your camp,' said the girl.

'Never!' said Raven. 'River Camp belongs to us.'

'We need it,' said the girl. 'This land belongs to us.'

Bear stepped forward too. 'No it doesn't. We were here first.'

'No,' said the girl. 'We were.'

'Prove it,' said Fox.

The girl jutted her chin out. 'We knew about you, before you knew about us.'

Raven started marching forward. 'You are not having River Camp. Come on, Mouse, jump down. The Ogre Tree is just a silly story to frighten you.'

The branches above Mouse creaked and groaned and they began to shake and bend towards Mouse. They looked like giant claws about to grab him. Sniff barked and backed away.

'Don't anger the Ogre Tree,' warned the girl. 'You don't want to wake the spirits of the forest.'

One of the boys stepped forward. 'Or the zombies in the Lake of the Dead will get you,' he said.

The pool lay dark and still between them. The forest was reflected in the water so perfectly that it looked to Willow as if there was another world inside the pool. As she leaned over, she could see pale white shapes glistening just beneath the surface, and she saw another Willow peer up at her.

The girl walked around the pool edge. Willow noticed her face was covered with moss and lichen. Her hands were green too.

'You're the one they call Willow, aren't you?' said the girl.

Willow nodded. 'And who are you?'

'I'm Hazel,' said the girl. 'We are the guardians of the forest.'

'The guardians,' echoed voices deep within the trees. 'The guardians. The guardians.'

Fox tried to look between the trees. 'How many

of you are there?'

'As many as there are trees in the forest,' said Hazel.

'You're just thieves,' said Raven. 'Where's Hare's compass and Fox's penknife? Where are our pots and pans too?'

'And the rest of our cookies,' said Bear. 'What have you done with them?'

'Very tasty,' said Hazel. 'You can make some more.'

Bear swiped at her, but she jumped aside.

'You can't have River Camp,' said Fox.

'Then you can't have Mouse back,' said Hazel. She stared at the rolled-up map in Hare's hand. 'Is that a map?'

'Might be,' said Hare.

'We want that too,' said Hazel.

Hare held the map against her chest. 'A map-maker never gives up her map.'

One of the boys stepped out from the shadows. 'We'll give you an hour to think about the map,' he said, 'or you say goodbye to Mouse.'

The tree above Mouse creaked and groaned again, and Sniff tucked himself behind Willow's legs and growled.

'Who are you?' said Fox to the boy.

'I'm Rowan,' said one boy.

'And I'm Ash,' said the other, stepping out too. 'There are lots of us, so you'd better come back and give up your camp and the map, or we'll find a way to take them anyway.'

Fox looked at Rowan and Ash and couldn't tell them apart. 'We'll be back,' he said. 'Don't worry, Mouse. We'll save you.'

The Wild Things headed back out of the Forest of Forever Night without Mouse.

'We have to get Mouse back,' said Willow.

'But how?' said Bear. 'You saw the Ogre Tree move. We won't get near him. And if he tries to escape, it'll flatten him.'

Raven scowled. 'We can't let them have River Camp.'

Hare held tightly onto the map. 'They can't have the map either.'

Fox stomped alongside Raven. 'You know what this means.'

They turned to look at him.

'What?' said Bear.

Fox looked grim. 'This means war.'

Chapter 6
Land of the Dragon

'But what can we do?' said Hare as they arrived back at River Camp. 'We don't know how many of them there are. They all look the same. They even have an Ogre Tree.'

Raven folded her cloak around her and frowned. 'Then we have to have something bigger to fight with,' she said.

Hare sat down and unrolled the map. 'I'm going to add in the Lake of the Dead and the Ogre Tree. At least we can find our way back to Mouse with the map if we have to.'

Willow crouched next to Hare and looked at the map. It was a huge map showing the places in the Wilderness that Hare had visited. There were blank unknown spaces too, waiting to be discovered. She peered closely at a picture of a dragon guarding a cave beside a round pool. It was labelled Dragon Gardens. Willow hadn't been there before. 'What's there?' she said.

'What do you think?' said Hare a little crossly.

'There's not really a dragon, is there?' said Willow.

Hare put her pencil down and looked up at her. 'Of course there is.'

'It lives in the grotto,' said Fox.

'What's a grotto?' asked Willow.

'The cave where it sleeps,' said Fox. 'We only went there once. We didn't actually see it, but we heard it and saw its dragon breath.'

Willow traced her fingers over the dragon on the map. 'How easy is it to train a dragon?'

Raven frowned. 'If we could train the dragon, we could get it to fight the Ogre Tree.'

Bear clapped his hands and laughed. 'The Ogre Tree would be charcoal after dragon fire.'

'But how do you train a dragon?' asked Willow.

Fox pointed a stick to a hut drawn on the map. 'There's only one person to ask.'

Raven nodded. 'The witch.'

The Wild Things set out for the witch's cottage. She lived in a hut in the wood between River Camp and the great swamp. She was a writer who had a writing hut in the woods, but the Wild Things suspected her of secretly being a witch. She had helped them before. Maybe she could help them now.

As they walked, Sniff seemed unsettled. He was growly and grumbly and kept looking back into the trees. Willow kept looking behind too, but she couldn't see anyone or anything. A campfire was smouldering outside the witch's hut, and a blue light glowed from within.

'CAW! CAW!' A large crow bobbed up and down on a branch next to them. 'CAW!'

The witch stuck her head outside. 'Who's there?'

'It's us,' said Raven. 'The Wild Things.'

'Are you busy?' asked Hare.

'I'm always busy,' said the witch.

'We've come to ask you about dragons,' said Fox. 'Can you help us?'

'Dragons, eh? Dangerous beasts!' The witch frowned and scratched her head. 'All right, I'll stoke up the fire.'

The Wild Things sat in a circle around the fire. Hare tucked the map behind her, well away from the flames and sparks that jumped out of the embers.

Raven tried to peer into the hut. 'Were you working on spells?'

The witch blocked the inside of the hut from view and closed the door. 'You know I don't do

spells as a rule. I write words to conjure portals into other worlds,' she said. 'If you must know, I was about to enter a pirate ship.'

'Cool,' said Bear. 'Can we come?'

'No,' said the witch. 'There's a pirate about to board my ship. I've left at a rather precarious moment.' She turned to Fox. 'So what's the problem?'

'There are strangers in the Wilderness,' said Fox. 'We don't want them here. This place is ours.'

The witch put her head on one side. 'Who says it belongs to you?'

Raven folded her arms. 'We were here first.'

'Hmm,' said the witch. 'How do you know that? And if you were, what makes you think you own this place?'

Fox frowned. 'Well, these strangers call themselves the Bark Skins. They say the

Wilderness is theirs. They've taken Mouse and will feed him to the Ogre Tree unless we give them River Camp.'

'And they want my map,' said Hare.

'They've eaten our cookies already,' said Bear.

'Hmm,' said the witch. 'Have you asked why they want your camp?'

'We shouldn't have to,' snapped Raven. 'It's ours.'

Fox scowled. 'It's war. We're going to fight them for it.'

'I see!' said the witch. 'I don't approve of wars. Wars are best fought with words, not weapons.'

'We hoped you'd help us train a dragon to fight the Ogre Tree,' said Willow.

'And where will you find a dragon?' said the witch.

'There's one that lives in Dragon Gardens,'

said Raven. 'The entrance is guarded by two stone dragons. We know all about it. We've been there before.'

'You mean the secret garden?' said the witch, scratching her chin. She gave a deep sigh. 'I wouldn't advise disturbing dragons. People underestimate them. They poke them with sticks and put chains on them. They think they can tame them, but they don't realize the power dragons can unleash, until it's too late.'

'What if we offered it gold?' said Raven. 'Dragons love gold.'

The witch shook her head. 'Never enter a contract with a dragon. You will be in its debt forever. There's only one way to control a dragon.'

'What's that?' said Fox.

The witch poked the fire and sparks flew up into the air. 'I could tell you, but it comes with a heavy warning.'

Sniff growled softly, the hackles on his neck rising.

'Shh, Sniff!' whispered Willow. She wanted to hear what the witch had to say.

The witch peered into the dark spaces between the trees. 'It has been said that, if you hold the dragon's egg, you can control the dragon. Dragons are known to sleep beside their eggs.'

'But how do you take an egg from a sleeping dragon?' said Fox.

'I believe you have to sing to keep it asleep,' said the witch. 'Dragons can sleep for over a hundred years, but they wake easily if there are egg thieves about.'

'And where would we find the dragon's egg?' said Bear.

'Where you find the dragon, of course,' said the witch.

The Wild Things looked at each other.

'The secret grotto,' said Hare. 'I've marked it on the map. We're sure there's a sleeping dragon there.'

'But there's something important you should know about a dragon's egg—' began the witch.

'UFF! UFF! UFF!' barked Sniff.

'Shh, Sniff!' said Willow. But then she saw what he was barking at. A pair of hands shot out from behind a bush and grabbed the map from behind Hare's back, then vanished. Footsteps slapping on the mud could be heard disappearing into the distance.

'The Bark Skins!' yelled Raven.

'They were listening to us all the time,' said Bear. 'They heard how to control the dragon.'

'They've got my map!' cried Hare. 'They're going to get the dragon egg before us.'

'We'll lose River Camp for good,' said Fox.

Raven leapt to her feet. 'Not if we get there first.'

Chapter 7
When the Singing Stops

'Wait!' cried the witch. 'There is something you should know about the dragon's egg.'

The Wild Things stopped. Fox tapped his foot impatiently.

'There is a dangerous price to pay. You can never put it down unless you want to give the dragon back its power. It is a heavy weight to bear,' said the witch. 'Because the dragon's egg has a power all of its own. You must use it wisely.'

Willow crept closer. 'What sort of power?'

'It depends upon the keeper of the egg,' said the witch. 'It holds the oldest magic. It is said that whatever you give to others will return to find you.'

'Come on!' yelled Raven, disappearing into the trees. 'We don't have time to talk.'

The Wild Things raced after Raven.

Sniff barked alongside Willow.

'I didn't listen to you, Sniff. You were trying to warn us the Bark Skins were there,' said Willow.

'Uff!' woofed Sniff.

The Wild Things followed Hare until they reached a tall ivy-covered wall.

'This wall goes all the way round Dragon Gardens,' whispered Hare. 'There's only one way in.' She pointed to two stone dragons either side of a door with flaked paint. The dragons were speckled orange with lichens and furred with green moss, but their mouths were open in silent roars.

'We're too late,' said Bear. 'The Bark Skins have beaten us to it. They're already inside.'

They could hear a tuneless song coming from the other side of the door.

'They're singing to the dragon to keep him asleep,' whispered Hare.

'That means it's not over yet,' said Willow. 'They haven't found the egg.'

The Wild Things slipped through the door and into Dragon Gardens. Willow just stopped and stared. The red-brick wall formed a square around an old garden. It was like a lost land of fairy tales. Trees grew tall and wild. Ivy crisscrossed the stone paths between flowerbeds that exploded in colours of different flowers. Old pear trees were heavy with fruit. Wasps buzzed about, feeding on the fallen pears. In the centre of the garden, a unicorn statue rose up above an ornate pond.

Willow walked closer. There had been a fountain once, but the pond was now green and filled with pondweed. She bent over and looked in. Something wriggled to the depths of the pond, disappearing amongst the weed. A newt! One of Freddie's dragons. Then she saw another and another.

Raven looked in too. 'Water boatman,' she said, pointing to a small insect swimming just beneath the surface, moving two of its long legs like rowing oars.

Hare joined them. 'Pond skaters too,' she said, watching another insect slide across the surface.

'It's like another world in there,' said Willow.

'Come on,' said Fox. 'We have to go to the grotto.'

'This way,' said Bear.

They followed the sound of the Bark Skins'

singing to a path that led down between rocks to the opening of the grotto. A stone bench had been placed next to a stream that trickled out of the grotto, spilling over rocks that glittered in the light.

The Bark Skins' singing came from deep in the cave.

'Has anyone got a torch?' whispered Willow.

The others shook their heads.

Sniff growled softly.

'Shh, Sniff,' whispered Willow. 'Stay outside and guard the entrance.'

'Let's go in together,' said Raven.

They all crept in and the darkness swallowed them up. Willow stood still, letting her eyes adjust to the dim light.

'How do we know if the dragon is in here?' said Hare.

'What do you think it looks like?' said Fox, peering into the darkness.

Willow stared hard. She was certain something moved. Maybe the flick of a tail. Maybe the shine of dragon scales. A cool mist hung in the air.

'What if it wakes?' whispered Bear.

'As long as someone keeps singing, we're safe,' said Hare. 'That's what the witch said.'

'Come on,' whispered Willow. 'Let's find the egg.'

Willow crept forward. She didn't realize she had left the others behind. She was following the small stream that glistened in the gloom.

She could hear the drip of water from the cave roof and the Bark Skins' song echoing off the walls.

The stream led to a shallow pool lit up by a shaft of light coming through a hole in the cave roof. The reflections from the water danced on the cave walls. Willow held her breath. There was a huge dragon lying in the centre of the pool, half submerged. It was pale and glittered in the shafts of light. The water shimmered around it, and in the gloom, Willow couldn't tell if it was made of stone or if it was a real dragon that was fast asleep. Then she saw what she was looking for amongst the stones in the pool.

It was smooth and round and it sparkled with crystals.

The dragon egg.

She bent forward to pick it up, but at that moment realized something was different.

It was eerily quiet.

The singing had stopped.

Something slid past her and bumped into her in the darkness. She stumbled to the ground and covered her head, ready for the dragon to attack.

But nothing happened.

When she looked up again, the dragon's egg was gone.

Chapter 8
Power of the Egg

Laughter echoed around the cave. It circled round and round making Willow's head spin.

'We have it, we have it!' sang a voice beside her.

Willow recognized the voice; it belonged to Hazel.

'We have the egg,' Hazel shouted triumphantly. 'We control the dragon and we demand River Camp as our prize.'

Ash and Rowan cheered from somewhere in the darkness.

Willow stumbled out of the cave to see Hazel

holding the dragon egg up high. Ash and Rowan joined her.

The other Wild Things just stared at the egg.

'I'm sorry, I almost got it,' Willow said. 'But Hazel grabbed it first.'

Fox shook his head. 'We'll have to give up River Camp.'

Hare glanced at the rolled-up paper in Ash's hand. 'They've got my map too.'

'We can't give it all up,' said Bear.

Raven sighed. 'We have no choice. We've lost. They control the dragon now.'

Hazel walked up to Fox. The egg glittered in the sunlight. 'Henceforth, the Wild Things are banished from this land, never to return. The Wilderness is ours. You can collect your friend and then go.'

'And never come back,' said Ash.

'Ever,' agreed Rowan. 'Or we'll wake the dragon and set it on you.'

Hazel led the way back through the woods to River Camp. She stood in the centre of River Camp and held the egg up high. 'River Camp is ours. We've beaten you, three of us against six of you.'

'There's only three of you?' said Fox.

'Yes,' laughed Ash.

'And we won the egg,' said Rowan. He held out his hand to Hazel. 'Can I hold it now?'

Hazel wrapped her fingers around the egg. She frowned and glanced sideways at Rowan. 'I found it. It's best that I look after it.'

'It belongs to us too,' said Ash.

'You might drop it,' said Hazel.

'I won't,' said Ash. 'I just want to hold it, that's all.'

Hazel held the egg against her chest. 'It's mine. I found it.'

'It belongs to the three of us,' said Rowan. 'Let Ash hold it if he wants to.'

Hazel narrowed her eyes at them. 'You're both ganging up on me, aren't you?' She backed away from them into the den. 'Well, I'm not giving it up. I'm in control of the dragon, and I control you too. Don't forget that.'

Willow glanced at the other Wild Things. It was as if the Bark Skins had forgotten they were there and were arguing amongst each other.

Ash pulled aside the tarpaulin. 'You're not in charge. I'm going home.'

Hazel stuck her head out. 'Go on then, go. I don't like you anymore.'

'I don't like you much either,' snapped Ash.

Hazel turned to Rowan. 'Let him go. He's

boring. It's you and me now.'

Rowan shook his head. 'It's no fun anymore. I'm going home too.'

'Come back!' yelled Hazel.

But Ash and Rowan disappeared into the trees of the Forest of Forever Night.

'What are you staring at?' snapped Hazel to the Wild Things.

Hare stared at the egg in Hazel's hand. 'The witch said the dragon egg had power. She said you had to use it wisely.'

Bear nodded. 'She said what you send out comes back to find you.'

'It's true,' said Raven. 'You've turned your friends against you. You said you didn't like them; now they don't like you.'

Hazel cradled the egg against her chest. 'It's not true,' she said. But her eyes shone with tears.

'Well, we'll leave you to have River Camp to yourself,' said Willow. 'It's what you wanted. We'll go and get Mouse.'

The Wild Things set off into the Forest of Forever Night. Willow glanced back once to see Hazel sitting in the middle of the camp, her shoulders slumped forward, just staring at the egg in her hands.

The Wild Things walked in silence to the Lake of the Dead.

Ash and Rowan were helping Mouse down from the tree.

'What happened?' said Mouse.

'We've lost River Camp,' said Raven. 'We've come to take you home.'

'We're going home too,' said Rowan. 'It's not much fun anymore.'

'We're sorry we took your cookies,' said Ash. He handed Hare the map. 'This belongs to you.'

Rowan reached into a bag beside the Ogre Tree and pulled out a penknife and compass. 'These are yours too. I'm sorry we took them.'

'And these,' said Ash fetching the pots and pans. 'We shouldn't have taken them.'

'Come on, Mouse,' said Willow. 'It's time to go.'

Mouse looked around. 'I don't want to leave the Wilderness. I love this place.'

Sniff licked his hand and whined.

'None of us want to leave, Mouse,' said Raven. 'But we've got no choice.'

'Wait!'

Ash, Rowan, and the Wild Things looked up to see Hazel running towards them.

She held the egg out to Willow. 'Take it,' she said.

Willow took the egg in her hands. It felt curiously cold and heavy.

'It's true,' Hazel said. 'It does have power.' She stared down at her feet. 'I wanted it for myself, and now I've turned my friends against me.'

Willow turned the egg over and over in her hands. She wasn't sure if she wanted to hold it either. 'Why did you want our camp anyway?'

The Bark Skins looked at each other, and a silence fell where only the gurgling of the stream could be heard.

'We had to leave our own camp deep in the forest,' said Hazel. 'We wanted to borrow your tools and things to make a new den, but it didn't work out. We didn't know how. So we thought it would be easier to have your camp instead.'

'But why did you have to leave your own camp?' asked Mouse.

Ash looked up. 'We had to leave because others moved in to our den.'

Raven's eyes opened wide. 'There are others in the woods? Not just you?'

'Well, they're—' began Rowan.

'Shh!' said Hazel, digging him in the ribs. 'Don't say.'

But it was too late. They had told their secret. There were others in the Wilderness too.

Chapter 9
No Place for Dragons

'This means we can have River Camp back,' said Bear, grinning.

Hazel nodded. 'It wasn't worth losing my friends over it.'

The Bark Skins started to walk away, heads down.

'But now they don't have anywhere to live,' said Hare.

The Wild Things looked at each other.

'We could help them,' said Mouse.

Willow nodded. 'We know how much we love

River Camp. We wouldn't want to lose it.'

'Time for a Wild Squawk,' said Fox.

The Wild Things gathered together and came up with a plan, and as they did, Willow could feel the egg grow warmer and warmer in her hands.

Fox turned to the Bark Skins. 'Wait!' he shouted. 'We've all decided that we could help you make a camp of your own in the forest.'

Hazel stopped and turned around. 'Really?'

'Yes, really,' said Raven. 'There's plenty of room here for us all.'

'Where do you want to make your den?' said Fox.

'We quite like it here, next to the Ogre Tree,' said Hazel. She pointed up into the branches. 'A tree house would be cool.'

Fox nodded. 'We'll need to collect some branches and ropes.'

'We've got some ropes of our own,' said Ash. He pointed to some long ropes attached to the branches higher up. 'We pulled on these to make the Ogre Tree move to scare you.'

Mouse shuddered. 'So, there wasn't an ogre or any zombies?'

Ash shrugged his shoulders. 'Is the stone dragon in the grotto a real dragon?'

'I'm sure it is,' said Hare.

'Have you seen it move?' asked Rowan.

Hare frowned. 'Just because we haven't seen it move, doesn't mean it's not real.'

'Come on,' said Fox. 'Let's make this tree house.'

Together the Wild Things and the Bark Skins heaved and hauled fallen branches up into the tree to make a platform between the low-spreading branches. Fox and Raven showed them how to tie

knots, and when they had finished, they sat high in the tree house, on a level with the birds.

Bear went off and came back with an old tyre which he tied from a branch, and all the Wild Things and Bark Skins took turns swinging on it.

'How do you disguise yourself to look like trees?' said Willow.

Hazel scooped some mud from a pot and worked some water into it. 'We make mud masks and paint it on our faces. It's how we make the tree faces too. We'll have to make a mud ogre face for the Ogre Tree.'

Willow helped Hazel shape mud into a face upon the tree, with stones as eyes and sticks and moss as a beard.

'This is so much better than our old den,' said Ash.

'Much better,' said Rowan. 'I don't think we

could go back there anyway.'

'Why not?' said Hare.

Hazel frowned and looked at Ash and Rowan.
'Shall we show them? I think we can trust them.
We owe them.'

Ash and Rowan nodded.

'Show us what?' asked Raven.

'The reason we had to leave our den,' said
Hazel. 'But first, we have to paint you with mud.'

Ash nodded. 'We can't risk being seen.'

Chapter 10
The Old Magic

The Wild Things had their faces painted with mud. Hazel said Willow had to hold Sniff and stop him from barking.

'We have to be quiet,' she said. 'We can't be seen or heard.'

The Wild Things followed the Bark Skins deeper and deeper into the forest. The trees grew close together, their trunks furred with moss. It created a strange green twilight.

'We have to stop here,' whispered Ash. He

pointed to an old tree lying on the ground. It was huge, an old fallen giant of the forest. It looked hollow inside.

'That was our den,' said Rowan. 'It was dry and warm inside, especially when it rained.'

'So who lives there now?' whispered Hare.

'Shh!' said Hazel. 'Just wait. And don't move a muscle.'

Willow sat quite still, her legs becoming numb and tingling where Sniff pressed heavily on her lap. They waited and waited. Her mind began to wander. Evening sunlight slanted through the trees and Willow realized it had got quite late. Her parents would be worrying, and she'd have to get home soon. She thought of Mum and Dad and Freddie and Nana in the neat garden, so different from the tangled trees of the Wilderness.

'Look,' whispered Mouse, nudging Willow.

Willow looked out where Mouse was
pointing. She couldn't see anything different.

'Look by the tree.'

Willow stared and then saw what Mouse
was pointing at. There was a face looking out.
And then another and then another.

Three round fluffy faces bobbed
up and down.

'Owls!' whispered Willow.

She turned to the others and grinned.

'They're about four weeks old,' whispered Hazel. 'When we discovered owls nesting, we knew we couldn't stay in our den. The owls needed it more than us.'

The Wild Things and the Bark Skins watched the owls from their safe distance as the shadows grew long across the ground.

'We have to go now,' said Hazel. 'The mother will be hunting soon, and we don't want to disturb her.'

'We have to go too,' said Raven.

They all scrambled back through the undergrowth to the Bark Skins' new den.

'You can't tell anyone about the owls,' said Hazel. 'Promise.'

'We wouldn't,' said Fox.

'People would come and disturb them if they found out,' said Ash.

'The forest is a home for the owls,' said Rowan. 'There's nowhere else where they can live in the city. Imagine if they were the last owls on earth.'

The Bark Skins stood facing the Wild Things beneath the boughs of the Ogre Tree.

'Thank you for building our tree house,' said Hazel. 'If you ever need our help, come and find us.'

'Same,' said Fox. 'We all need to protect this place.'

'We're all guardians of the Wilderness,' said Raven.

The Wild Things headed back to their homes.

They passed River Camp on their way and returned the map, penknife, and compass to their den.

Willow held out the egg in her hands. 'Maybe it does hold the old magic,' she said. 'We shared our help, and the Bark Skins shared their secret with us.'

'You're right,' said Mouse. 'I've always wanted to see owls.'

'I think we should take the egg back to the dragon,' said Willow. 'It doesn't seem right to keep it.'

The Wild Things slipped back through the wooden door into Dragon Gardens.

'It might be angry that we took its egg,' whispered Mouse.

'We'll have to sing to keep it asleep,' said Bear.

Willow stepped into the grotto holding the egg out in front of her while Bear hummed a tune.

The dragon lay coiled and sleeping in the light

from the hole in the cave roof.

Willow gently placed the egg where she found it, and they walked back out into the sunlight.

'I wonder how long the dragon's been here,' said Mouse. 'How long has it been asleep?'

'Maybe dragons don't like living in cities,' said Raven. 'Maybe it's the last dragon on earth.'

Willow felt a sadness wash over her. She thought of Freddie's newt and wondered where it would go if it lost its home. What if all the creatures were driven out of their homes? Dragon Gardens were lost in time, somehow. They held the dragon, but they also held the deep green ponds filled with strange and wonderful creatures.

'We can't tell anyone about this place,' said Hare. She pulled out her map and her rubber-tipped pencil and began to rub out the dragon on her map. 'It has to stay secret for always, to protect it.'

Bear pulled the door closed after them, and the Wild Things covered the door and the dragons guarding the entrance with loose branches and ivy so that no one could see the way in. 'I love the Wilderness,' he said. 'We have so many adventures here. Who would've thought we'd make friends with the Bark Skins and see owls too!'

'Come on,' said Raven. 'It's getting dark and we'd better get back.'

Fox looked up at the clouds tinged red with the setting sun. 'I wonder what it's like to spend a night in the forest with the owls and darkness. I wonder what adventures we'd have then.'

Hare nodded. 'Next time. We'll do it next time.'

The Wild Things lost their wild look outside the Wilderness. Raven's wings drooped in cloth around her shoulders. Fox seemed less foxy, and Bear seemed smaller somehow. Hare walked instead of bounced, and Mouse's nose stopped twitching.

'Goodbye Willow Wildthing,' said Raven.

'Goodbye,' said Fox.

'Goodbye,' said Bear.

'Goodbye,' said Mouse.

'Until next time,' said Hare.

'Goodbye,' said Willow.

'Uff!' barked Sniff.

Willow watched them walk away down the path.

They were going back to their homes and their families too.

Willow looked back into the woodland that had held dragons and owls. It was a small patch of green in the vast city. It was a wild place for the Wild Things to escape to. A small wilderness that some animals and the Wild Things called home.

Chapter 11
Releasing the Dragon

Willow hurried home and slipped under the hedge with Sniff bounding ahead of her. She walked into the kitchen where Mum and Nana were having a cup of tea, and Freddie was in a high chair, eating his supper. Dad was lying on the kitchen floor, groaning.

Willow stepped over him, and Sniff wagged his tail and pushed his nose in Dad's face.

'Where have you been?' said Mum. 'I was about

to come and look for you.'

'I was out with friends,' said Willow.

'I don't like you going into that bit of wasteland,' said Mum.

'It's fun,' said Willow. 'I was with friends. We made some new friends too.'

'Dragon,' said Freddie, pointing to the newt in the glass tank.

Mum rolled her eyes. 'Freddie's obsessed with Mr Tickles. He wants to take his dragon everywhere with him. He won't leave it alone.'

Dad tried to sit up but groaned again.

'What's wrong with Dad?' whispered Willow.

'He's done too much digging,' said Mum. 'He's given himself a bad back.'

Dad pulled himself up and leaned on the table. 'I'll have to get someone in to dig up those bushes.'

'Please don't,' said Willow.

Dad looked up. 'Someone will have to do it.'

Willow pulled the glass tank closer to her and looked in. She could see the newt tucked under a stick amongst some dry leaves. It was very still. She thought of the newts she had seen swimming free in Dragon Gardens. 'It'll get sick,' she said. 'It'll die in here.'

Freddie looked at Willow's sad face, and his lower lip stuck out and wobbled.

'It's Freddie's zoo,' said Nana. 'You can't take it away from him now.'

Willow gently scooped the newt in her hand. 'It doesn't belong in a zoo,' she said. 'It belongs in the wild. If we dig up its home, it won't have anywhere to live. It won't be able to find any other newts and we won't have any more newts. Ever.'

Nana slurped her tea. 'It isn't going to make any difference if we dig up one garden or not.'

'Isn't it?' said Willow. 'What if everyone says that? What if everyone covered their gardens in concrete? What if everyone cut their lawns and dug up the wild plants? There'd be no room for wildlife.'

'But it's a mess out there,' said Dad. 'We'll have to clear up the weeds.'

'People only call them weeds because they don't want them,' said Willow. 'But the animals need them. Mr Tickles will die in this tank.'

Freddie began to cry. Big fat tears rolled down his cheeks.

'Now look,' said Nana. 'Freddie's getting upset.'

'We have to let the newt go,' said Willow. 'We can't dig up its home. Please don't, Dad. Imagine if someone came and dug up our home. Where would we go? Where would we live?'

Dad frowned. 'We have plans for a summer

house and a hot tub.'

'We can have a pond instead,' said Willow. 'Then we can have lots of newts. We can have water boatmen and pond skaters too. Freddie and I can watch frogs and tadpoles.' She turned to Freddie. 'Do you want lots of newts in the garden?'

Freddie nodded. 'Dragons,' he said.

Willow laughed. 'We'll have lots of dragons. Wild dragons.'

'I don't know,' said Dad. 'I'm not sure what the neighbours would think if we left it a mess.'

'We can leave the end of the garden wild, for Freddie and me,' pleaded Willow. 'It'll be our garden. Our wild garden. We can put up bird feeders too.'

Mum poured herself another cup of tea. 'A pond would be cheaper than a hot tub.'

Dad sighed. 'Less work too, I suppose,' he said.

'When my back's a bit better, I'll start digging a hole for a pond. A big one.'

'You'll need a fence around it while Freddie is young,' said Nana. Nana always liked to point out dangers.

'So we can keep it like it is?' said Willow.

'I suppose so,' said Dad.

'Just don't go bringing the wildlife inside,' said Mum.

'We won't,' said Willow. She hauled Freddie out from his high chair. 'Come on, we're going to release your dragon.'

She walked with Freddie down to the bottom of the garden, holding the newt in her hand. The grass was beaded with dew, and the evening light was soft and hazy blue. She put the newt into Freddie's hand. 'Here,' she said, holding it out to Freddie. 'You let it go.'

Freddie held the newt cupped in his hands. He didn't want to let it go. He wanted to keep it.

'He needs to go home, Freddie,' said Willow. 'We'll see him again.'

Freddie lowered his hands and let the newt scuttle away. It gave one last flick of its tail before it disappeared beneath the leaves.

'Home now,' said Freddie.

Willow smiled. 'Home now.'

Freddie sat down in the wet grass. 'Dragon gone.'

'One day, we'll have lots of them here,' said Willow. 'Just you wait.'

'Willow!' called Mum. 'Time for you both to come in.'

'In a minute,' Willow called back. She lay down in the long grass and breathed in the cool evening air. A ladybird tiptoed on its six legs to the tip of a blade of grass. It opened its spotted wings and took flight. She watched its small shape disappear into the dusky sky.

There were little pockets of wilderness everywhere if you looked for them, Willow thought. Adults just couldn't seem to see them. They wanted neat, tidy places they could keep under control. They wanted to put animals in cages and zoos. But wild animals belonged in the wild. She tried to imagine a tidy world with no wilderness and no wildlife. Neat and tidy was definitely dull and boring. The wild was tangled, untamed, and full of extraordinary surprises.

Freddie lay down next to her, and she put her arms around him.

'You'll love the Wilderness, Freddie,' whispered Willow. 'We'll have so many adventures together. You and me. I can't wait to take you there one day

and meet the Wild Things. One day I'll take you
to Dragon Gardens too.'

Sniff snuggled down between them. Evening
mist settled on the trees like dragon breath, and as
the first star appeared above the Wilderness,
an owl hooted three times into the night.

How to make a tree face!

You can make your own tree face out of mud, just like the Bark Skins! Ask an adult to help you find soil that is safe to use. (You can also use air-dry clay instead of mud.)

You will need:

- water
- bucket
- strong stick
- moss, leaves, twigs, small stones
- soil (or air-dry clay)

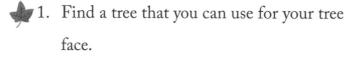

 1. Find a tree that you can use for your tree face.

 2. Mix your mud.

Put some soil into the bucket. Slowly add some water and stir with your stick. Add more soil or water until you have thick mud which can stick to your tree trunk. (If you are using air-dry clay, knead it on a hard surface to soften it.)

 3. Squish the mud (or clay) on to the tree trunk in the shape of a face.

4. Press your moss, leaves, twigs, and stones into the mud (or clay) to add the details of your tree face. Use moss or leaves for a beard, twigs for eyebrows, and stones for eyes. Get creative!

 5. Don't forget to wash your hands!

Written by Gill Lewis

Willow Wildthing
and the
Swamp Monster

Illustrated by Rebecca Bagley

When Willow meets the Wild Things
she knows her life is never going to be
the same again. Strange things happen in
The Wilderness. It holds more than you
could possibly imagine: secrets, shadows,
a witch. Even a monster. Are you brave
enough to come . . . ?

Gill Lewis spent much of her childhood in the garden, where she ran a small zoo and a veterinary hospital for creepy-crawlies, mice, and birds. When she grew up, she became a real vet and travelled from the Arctic to Africa in search of interesting animals and places.

Gill now writes books for children. Her previous novels have published to worldwide critical acclaim and have been translated into more than twenty languages.

She lives in the depths of Somerset with her husband and three children and writes from a tree house in the company of squirrels.

Rebecca Bagley is a children's book illustrator in the south-west of England.

Illustrators are funny sort of grown-ups. They do grown-up things, like brushing their teeth (every day), but they also sit around drawing pictures and then call it a job. Recently, Rebecca has been drawing a lot of leaves, as well as all the magical things that live amongst them, and she couldn't be happier about it.

In between drawings, Rebecca daydreams about having her own garden one day, where she will grow tomatoes, practise handstands, and have a really big dog. Until then, she entertains herself and her little family by feeding new and weird flavours to her baby girl who, so far, has been a very good sport.

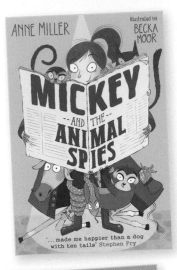

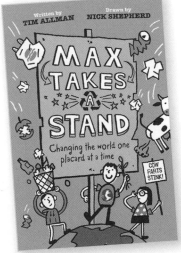